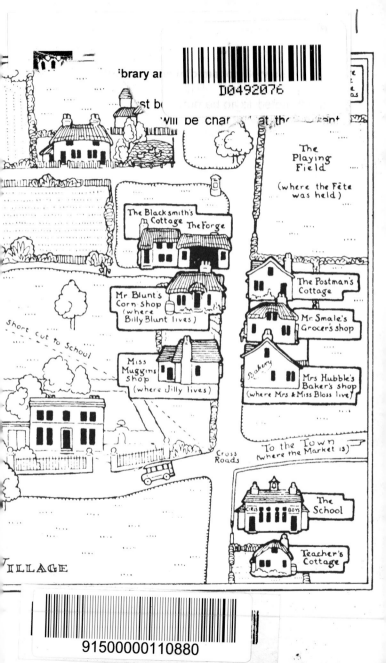

The Playing Field

(where the Fête was held)

The Blacksmith's Cottage

The Forge

The Postman's Cottage

Mr Blunt's Corn Shop (where Billy Blunt lives)

Mr Smale's Grocer's shop

Short cut to school

Miss Muggins Shop (where Jilly lives)

Bakery

Mrs Hubble's Baker's shop (where Mrs & Miss Bloss live)

To the Town (where the Market is)

Cross Roads

GIRLS   BOYS

The School

Teacher's Cottage

VILLAGE

MILLY-
MOLLY-
MANDY'S
Winter

Milly-Molly-Mandy books

Joyce Lankester Brisley

MILLY-MOLLY-MANDY'S

Winter

MACMILLAN CHILDREN'S BOOKS

The stories in this collection first appeared in
Milly-Molly-Mandy Stories (1928)
Further Doings of Milly-Molly-Mandy (1932)
Milly-Molly-Mandy and Billy Blunt (1967)
Published by George G. Harrap & Co. Ltd

This edition published 2012 by Macmillan Children's Books
a division of Macmillan Publishers Limited
20 New Wharf Road, London N1 9RR
Basingstoke and Oxford
Associated companies throughout the world
www.panmacmillan.com

ISBN 978-1-4472-0803-7

A CIP catalogue record for this book is available from the British Library.

Contents

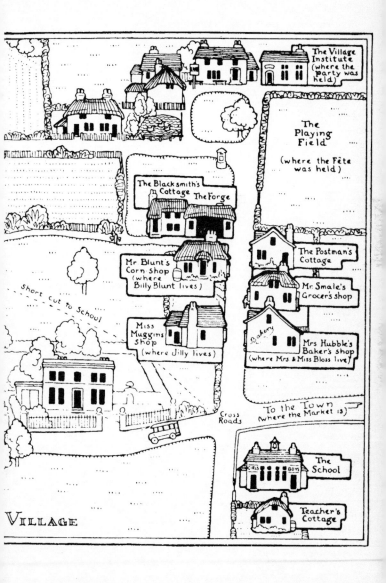

The Village Institute (where the party was held)

The Playing Field (where the Fête was held)

The Blacksmith's Cottage The Forge

The Postman's Cottage

Mr Blunt's Corn Shop (where Billy Blunt lives)

Mr Smale's Grocer's shop

Short cut to School

Miss Muggins Shop (where Jilly lives)

Bakery

Mrs Hubble's Baker's shop (where Mrs & Miss Bloss live)

To the Town (where the Market is)

Cross Roads

GIRLS   BOYS

The School

VILLAGE

Teacher's Cottage

Milly-Molly-Mandy Goes Visiting

Once upon a time Milly-Molly-Mandy had a letter. It was from Mrs Hooker, who had been a friend of Mother's ever since she was a little girl. And it said how sorry Mrs Hooker was to have to put Milly-Molly-Mandy off last time she had invited her – that time Milly-Molly-Mandy had enjoyed little-friend-Susan's visit instead of her own. But now Mrs Hooker's son and his wife had gone abroad to live, and Mrs Hooker would be very pleased if Mother would let Milly-Molly-Mandy come and spend a week-end with her, as promised.

Milly-Molly-Mandy was very pleased, and Father and Mother and Grandpa and Grandma and Uncle and Aunty were very pleased for her. They talked of Milly-Molly-Mandy going away nearly all supper-time, and Aunty promised to put a new ribbon round her best hat, and Mother said she must make her a very nice "going-away" nightdress in a case, and Uncle said he would feel very honoured if she were to borrow his small leather bag to take it in, and Father gave her sixpence to put in her purse.

Milly-Molly-Mandy felt so excited!

When Saturday morning came Grandpa got the pony-trap ready to go to market as usual, and Milly-Molly-Mandy came skipping down the path, ready to go with him and meet Mrs Hooker as arranged. Her hat looked just like new, and she had on a pair of nice warm woolly gloves that

Grandma had knitted for her, and Aunty's best nice warm woolly scarf, lent for the occasion.

Mother gave her a bunch of late chrysanthemums and a cream cheese for Mrs Hooker, with her love. And then Grandpa got up in the trap and took the reins, and Milly-Molly-Mandy was lifted up beside him. Then off trotted Twinkletoes, and Father and Mother and Grandma and Uncle and Aunty called, "Good-bye, Milly-Molly-Mandy! Have a nice time!" and waved, and Milly-Molly-Mandy waved back till she couldn't see them any longer. And she was really off for her visit!

They didn't see little-friend-Susan or Billy Blunt as they drove through the village, but Milly-Molly-Mandy waved at their houses, in case they might see her. And then they were out in the open country, and Milly-Molly-Mandy was glad of Aunty's nice warm woolly scarf and her own nice warm woolly gloves.

They came to the town, and got down by the big clock in the market-place, and Mrs Hooker came hurrying up, looking quite different, somehow (for Milly-Molly-Mandy had seen her only once before, and had nearly forgotten what she looked like).

And then Grandpa kissed Milly-Molly-Mandy good-bye, and went off to do his business in the market. And Milly-Molly-Mandy took Mrs Hooker's hand in its grey kid glove, and went off with her.

Milly-Molly-Mandy had never been away from home to stay before without either Father or Mother or Grandpa or Grandma or Uncle or Aunty, and it

"Good-bye, Milly-Molly-Mandy! Have a nice time!"

felt so strange and exciting.

"Well, Milly-Molly-Mandy," said Mrs Hooker, "I just want to buy some crochet-cotton, and then we will be getting home."

So they went into a big draper's shop, heaps of times bigger than Miss Muggins's shop at home, and Mrs Hooker asked for crochet-cotton. And while she was buying it Milly-Molly-Mandy looked about and felt the purse in her pocket. Presently she saw some pretty little guards to put over the points of knitting-needles, which she thought would be so useful to Grandma.

And suddenly Milly-Molly-Mandy had an idea: What fun it would be to take presents home for everybody! She had five pennies of her own as well as the sixpence Father had given her.

She wondered what everybody would like, and remembered Mother once saying, "Handkerchiefs always make an

6

acceptable present." So when she had
bought the guards for Grandma she asked
the lady behind the counter if she had any
handkerchiefs that weren't at all expensive,
and the lady behind the counter brought out
a boxful, each one marked with a letter in
one corner. So Milly-Molly-Mandy looked
at them all, and chose one for Mother with
"M" in the corner, and one for Aunty with
"A" in the corner. And then she had only
two pennies left. She wondered whatever
she could get for Father and Grandpa and
Uncle with twopence.

Presently Mrs Hooker finished her
purchases, and they went out into the
street to go to Mrs Hooker's house. There
were such a lot of people, all over the
pavement and road, for it was market-
day, and there seemed so much to look at
that Milly-Molly-Mandy wished she had
a dozen pairs of eyes. But still, with only

two, she managed to keep one on the shop-windows as they passed, hoping to see something which Father and Grandpa and Uncle might like. And suddenly she saw a tray of pink sugar mice in a sweet-shop, labelled "Two a penny."

"Oh, Mrs Hooker!" said Milly-Molly-Mandy, "would you mind waiting a moment while I get a sugar mouse to take home to Farver and Grandpa and Uncle?"

So Mrs Hooker held the leather bag and chrysanthemums and cream cheese until

Milly-Molly-Mandy came out with a bag of sugar mice in her hand (she had bought four, and once was to be a good-bye present for Mrs Hooker). She wished she could get presents for little-friend-Susan and Billy Blunt, but that didn't seem possible, for she had used up all her money.

When they got to Mrs Hooker's house they put the chrysanthemums in a vase on the table, and the cream cheese in a dish on the sideboard. (Mrs Hooker was very pleased with them.) And then there was just time before dinner for Milly-Molly-Mandy to unpack her small leather bag in the little room she was to sleep in all by herself. And she found Mother had popped in Booby Rabbit, the toy she had won at a party once, and had slept with ever since. She was so glad to see him, and hid him in her nightdress-case so that he shouldn't be seen, because he hadn't been invited. (It was such fun for Booby Rabbit!)

The plates at dinner were so pretty – quite different from the ones they had at home – and so were the wall-paper and the carpet. Altogether, there seemed so much to think about that there wasn't time to say much more than "Yes, please," and "No, thank you." But she enjoyed her dinner very much.

After dinner Mrs Hooker said, "I have asked Milly next door to come and spend the afternoon with you, and you can play with my old toys."

Milly-Molly-Mandy was very interested. And then she said, "Will Milly-next-door put her hat and coat on to come here?" – for their nearest neighbours at home were little-friend-Susan and the Moggses, and they lived five minutes' walk down the road (but only three minutes if you ran).

Mrs Hooker said she really couldn't

say. And presently the next-door gate squeaked, and then Mrs Hooker's gate squeaked, and then the door-bell rang, and Milly-next-door came in (with a coat on and no hat).

Mrs Hooker told Milly-Molly-Mandy to take Milly-next-door upstairs to her little room, to take her coat off. So Milly-Molly-Mandy played hostess, and let Milly-next-door use her comb, and asked her if her name was really Millicent Margaret Amanda, like Milly-Molly-Mandy's own. And Milly-next-door said no, it was Mildred.

Then Milly-next-door admired the new nightdress-case lying on the bed, and when Milly-Molly-Mandy showed her the new nightdress inside (which was pink) Milly-next-door admired that too. (She didn't see Booby Rabbit.) But when Milly-Molly-Mandy showed her the handkerchiefs marked "M" for Mother and "A" for Aunty Milly-next-door was quite surprised.

"Oh," said Milly-next-door, "my mother never has her handkerchiefs marked 'M'! She has them marked 'R', because her other name's Rose. What's your mother's other name?"

"It's Polly," said Milly-Molly-Mandy, in a sad little voice.

"Oh, well," said Milly-next-door comfortingly, "I expect they can use them, even if they aren't quite proper."

But Milly-Molly-Mandy didn't feel very comforted, for she had so wanted to give Mother and Aunty proper presents.

Then they went downstairs and played all the afternoon with Mrs Hooker's funny old-fashioned toys. And when the lamps were lit Mrs Hooker brought out a beautiful paint-box and a fashion-paper full of little girls, and Milly-Molly-Mandy and Milly-next-door each painted a little girl very carefully, and cut it out with Mrs Hooker's scissors, and gave it to each other for a keepsake.

And during tea Milly-Molly-Mandy had another good idea: she would paint and cut out some paper dolls, very, very nicely, and take them home to little-friend-Susan for a present! Milly-Molly-Mandy didn't think Billy Blunt would care for paper dolls; she didn't know what she could give him. She wished she had another ha'penny for a sugar mouse.

And now it was time for Milly-next-door to put on her coat again and go home. Milly-Molly-Mandy and she said good-bye, and promised to write to each other and exchange paper dolls.

Milly-Molly-Mandy had never slept all alone before, and when bedtime came she felt quite pleased and excited. Mrs Hooker came and tucked her in, and she admired her new nightdress. Booby Rabbit was under the bedclothes, but he couldn't resist coming up for a peep at Mrs Hooker, and Mrs Hooker saw him and stroked his ears, and said she would certainly have invited him if she had thought he cared to come. And then she kissed Milly-Molly-Mandy good night, and Milly-Molly-Mandy lay in the dark and enjoyed going to sleep in a different bed.

Sunday was a nice day. They went to church in the morning, and in the afternoon Milly-Molly-Mandy painted the paper dolls for little-friend-Susan.

And then came Monday, and Milly-Molly-Mandy's visit was over. It was in the afternoon that Grandpa and Twinkletoes came with the trap to fetch her home.

She was all ready but for slipping the sugar mouse on to the mantelshelf with a note, "With Love from M. M. M.", where Mrs Hooker would see it when she came in from seeing Milly-Molly-Mandy off; and then Milly-Molly-Mandy was perched in her seat beside Grandpa.

And just as they drove off Mrs Hooker put a little packet of chocolate in Milly-Molly-Mandy's lap, to eat on the way home, and they cried "Good-bye!" to each other, and waved, and soon Twinkletoes' twinkling feet had carried them right out of sight.

Presently Milly-Molly-Mandy, sitting in the trap, had yet another good idea; she could give the little packet of chocolate to Billy Blunt for a present!

So she said, "Grandpa, would you be very disappointed if we didn't eat this chocolate?" adding in a whisper, "I've got something in my bag for you!"

And Grandpa said, "Milly-Molly-

Mandy, I'm just feeling too excited to eat any chocolate now!"

So when they got home to the nice white cottage with the thatched roof, and Milly-Molly-Mandy had hugged Father and Mother and Grandpa and Grandma and Uncle and Aunty, she opened the leather bag, and gave:

Father a sugar mouse – and Father was pleased!

And Mother a handkerchief, marked "M" for Mother. But when Mother saw it she said, "Oh, how nice to have it all ready marked 'M' for Mary!" And Milly-Molly-Mandy suddenly remembered Mother's real name was Mary, and she was only called Polly "for short"! Milly-Molly-Mandy was so relieved that she had to jump up and down several times.

And then she gave Grandpa a sugar mouse – and Grandpa was pleased!

And Grandma the guards for her knitting-needles – and Grandma was pleased!

And Uncle a sugar mouse – and Uncle was pleased!

And Aunty a handkerchief marked "A" for Aunty. But when Aunty saw it she said, "How nice! mine is marked too – 'A' for Alice!" And Milly-Molly-Mandy suddenly remembered that Aunty and Alice both began with the same letter, and she was so very relieved that she had to jump up and down a great many times.

Next morning she ran down the road to little-friend-Susan's and gave her the painted paper dolls, and little-friend-Susan was pleased!

And later in the day she saw Billy Blunt, and gave him the little packet of chocolate – and Billy Blunt was very surprised, and pleased too, and he made her eat half, and it was the bigger half.

And then Milly-Molly-Mandy wrote a little letter to say "thank you" to Mrs Hooker.

Milly-Molly-Mandy just does enjoy going away visiting!

Milly-Molly-Mandy
Does an Errand

Once upon a time Milly-Molly-Mandy went on an errand to the Village. (It was only to get a tin of cocoa which Mother had forgotten to order.)

When she came to the grocer's shop Mr Smale the grocer was outside his door, opening up a box of kippers. (Kippers do smell rather kippery, so Milly-Molly-Mandy guessed Mr Smale

preferred to keep them outside – where people passing could see them too: he didn't often sell kippers.)

While Milly-Molly-Mandy waited till he had done, someone came out of the baker's shop next door, carrying a heavy shopping-basket and an umbrella, as well as a loaf of bread.

It was one of the Miss Thumbles, who lived in a cottage by the duck-pond. There were two Miss Thumbles, sisters, both so alike that the only way Milly-Molly-Mandy could tell them apart was that one always seemed to wear a hat, even to go in the garden. That was Miss Thumble. The other one, of course, was the Other Miss Thumble.

But today, being rather cold and windy, this Miss Thumble wore a warm woolly scarf tied over her grey hair. So Milly-Molly-Mandy really couldn't be sure whether she were Miss Thumble or the Other Miss Thumble.

Seeing the newly opened box of kippers, Miss Thumble (or perhaps it was the Other Miss Thumble) stopped and said:

"Dear me! I should like a couple of those – my sister does enjoy a nice grilled kipper for her tea! – But how I'm going to manage to carry everything—"

Mr Smale quickly clapped two flat glistening brown kippers together and went into the shop to wrap them up. So Milly-Molly-Mandy said:

"Shall I carry your bread for you?"

And she took it, while Miss Thumble thankfully put her basket down on the step to find her purse, and went inside to pay.

As Milly-Molly-Mandy waited there, with the loaf of bread and the basket, who should look over the Blunts' garden gate opposite but Billy Blunt! He came out and strolled across the road, hands in pockets.

"Hullo! That's not your basket," said Billy Blunt.

"No," said Milly-Molly-Mandy. "It's Miss Thumble's. I'm helping to carry her things."

"You can't carry that," said Billy Blunt.

"Yes, I can," said Milly-Molly-Mandy. "Some of it."

"It's too heavy," said Billy Blunt.

Milly-Molly-Mandy rather hoped he was going to offer to help too. But he only turned and went back in at the garden gate, just as Miss Thumble came out of the shop.

She thanked Milly-Molly-Mandy for keeping an eye on her basket, and tried to find room in it for the parcel of kippers. But one thing and another kept falling out – potatoes and cheese and a big round cabbage – rolling about on the pavement.

Milly-Molly-Mandy picked them up, very nearly dropping the loaf at the same time.

"Here, give 'em here," said Billy Blunt.

He had come out again, pulling his little old box-on-wheels with him.

Putting the heavy basket into it, with all the odd potatoes and kippers and things, he set off hauling it along the road, past the forge and round by the duck-pond, Milly-Molly-Mandy following hugging the loaf, and Miss Thumble stumping after them looking as pleased as anything!

By the little cottages they stopped, and Miss Thumble rattled the letter-box of one. And presently the door opened; and there was the other Miss Thumble, wearing felt slippers *and* a hat. (So Milly-Molly-Mandy knew *she* must be Miss Thumble, and the first one *was* the Other Miss Thumble.)

They all helped to pile the things on to the kitchen table, and both the Miss Thumbles were very grateful at having so much kind help.

"I know my sister finds the shopping very heavy at times," said Miss Thumble.

"But I don't usually have quite so much to carry all at once!" said the Other Miss Thumble.

She opened one of the packages for her sister to offer the visitors each a biscuit before they left. And though Billy Blunt wasn't too keen on oatmeal biscuits he took one and said thank you nicely, and so did

Sat down to enjoy their kippers

Milly-Molly-Mandy. (She liked all kinds of biscuits – but some more than others, of course!)

They walked, munching together, back with the empty cart as far as the Blunts' gate.

Billy Blunt said, "We'd better see if they'd like us to carry their shopping for them other times."

"Yes, let's!" said Milly-Molly-Mandy. "They haven't anyone to run errands for them."

And then she suddenly remembered her own errand!

And she said good-bye to Billy Blunt and ran across the road to the grocer's to get the tin of cocoa for Mother. (The kippers, she noticed, were nearly sold out already.)

When she got home to the nice white cottage with the thatched roof she told

Mother all about the Miss Thumbles, and also about the kippers at the grocer's. Mother said:

"Yes! Father happened to be passing, and he saw them too. He's just bought a dozen."

So that evening, when Father and Mother and Grandpa and Grandma and Uncle and Aunty sat down to enjoy their kippers (Milly-Molly-Mandy had half a one, with the bones carefully picked out, on a slice of toast) they liked to think of Miss Thumble and the Other Miss Thumble enjoying their kippers too!

Milly-Molly-Mandy Goes Carol-Singing

Once upon a time Milly-Molly-Mandy heard some funny sounds coming from the little garden at the side of Mr Blunt's corn-shop.

So she looked over the palings, and what should she see but Billy Blunt, looking very solemn and satisfied, blowing away on a big new shiny mouth-organ!

Milly-Molly-Mandy said, "Hullo, Billy!" And Billy Blunt blew "Hullo!" into his mouth-organ (at least, Milly-Molly-Mandy guessed it was that), and went on playing.

Milly-Molly-Mandy waited a bit and listened, and suddenly she found she knew what he was playing. "It's *Good King Wenceslas*!" said Milly-Molly-Mandy, "Isn't it? Can I have a go soon?"

"I'm practising," said Billy Blunt, stopping for a moment and then going on again.

"Practising what?" said Milly-Molly-Mandy.

"Carols," said Billy Blunt.

"What for?" said Milly-Molly-Mandy.

"Don't know," said Billy Blunt, "only it's Christmas time."

"Then we could go caroling!" said Milly-Molly-Mandy, with a sudden thought.

"You could play on your mouth-organ, and I could sing. We could do it outside people's houses on Christmas Eve. Ooh, let's!"

But Billy Blunt only said "Huh!" and went on blowing his mouth-organ. But he did it rather thoughtfully.

Milly-Molly-Mandy waited a bit longer, and then she was just going to say good-bye when Billy Blunt said, "Here! You can have a go if you want to."

So Milly-Molly-Mandy, very pleased, took the mouth organ and wiped it on her skirt, and had quite a good "go" (and Billy Blunt knew she was playing *God Save the King*). And then she wiped it again and gave it back saying, "Good-bye, Billy. Don't forget about the carol-singing," and went on homeward up the white road with the hedges each side.

A few days later (it was the day before

Christmas Eve) Billy Blunt came up to the nice white cottage with the thatched roof, where Milly-Molly-Mandy lived, to bring a bag of meal which Uncle had ordered from Mr Blunt's corn-shop for his chickens. Milly-Molly-Mandy was watching Father cut branches of holly from the holly-tree; but when she saw Billy Blunt she thought of the carols, and came running down to the path.

"I say," said Billy Blunt. "About that carol-singing."

"Yes!" said Milly-Molly-Mandy. "Have you been practising hard?"

"Mmm," said Billy Blunt, "I thought we might try 'em over now, if you're still keen on it. Where'll we do it?"

So Milly-Molly-Mandy led the way to

the barn; and there in private they made plans and tried over one or two songs. They couldn't do *Hark the Herald Angels Sing* or *Christians Awake*, as the top notes in both of them went beyond the top of the mouth-organ and Billy Blunt wouldn't sing the top notes, because he said it didn't sound proper. But he could play *Noël* and *While Shepherds Watched* and *Wenceslas* beautifully. So Milly-Molly-Mandy sang while Billy Blunt played, until they could do it together quite nicely.

"I'll have to ask Mother first if I may," said Milly-Molly-Mandy then. So they went round the back way into the kitchen, where Mother and Grandma and Aunty were mixing the Christmas pudding, and Milly-Molly-Mandy asked her question.

Just at first Mother looked a little doubtful. And then she said, "You know Christmas-time is giving time. If you don't mean to knock at the doors and sing for money—"

Milly-Molly-Mandy said, "No, we won't."

"Why, that would be very nice, then," said Mother, "if you do it as nicely as ever you can."

"We'll do it our very best, just for love," said Milly-Molly-Mandy; and Billy Blunt nodded. Then Mother gave them some almonds and bits of peel-sugar, and then Billy Blunt had to go back.

The next day, directly tea was over, Milly-Molly-Mandy, very excited, slipped out of the house in her coat and muffler, and ran down to the gate to look for Billy Blunt.

It was very dark. Presently she saw a bicycle lamp coming along the road. It was jogging up and down in a queer way for a bicycle. And then as it came near it started

waving to and fro, and Milly-Molly-Mandy
guessed there must be Billy Blunt with it;
and she skipped up and down outside the
gate, because it did look so exciting
and Christmassy!

"You ready? Come on,"
said Billy Blunt, and
the two of them set
off down the road.

Soon they came
to the Moggses'
cottage, and began
their carols. At the

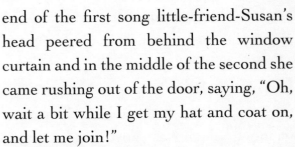

end of the first song little-friend-Susan's
head peered from behind the window
curtain and in the middle of the second she
came rushing out of the door, saying, "Oh,
wait a bit while I get my hat and coat on,
and let me join!"

And Mrs Moggs called from inside,
"Susan, bring them in quickly and shut

that door, you're chilling the house!"

So they hurried inside and shut the door; and there was Mrs Moggs sitting by the fire with Baby Moggs in her lap, and Mr Moggs was fixing a bunch of holly over the mantelpiece. Mrs Moggs gave them each a lump of toffee, and then Milly-Molly-Mandy and Billy Blunt with little-friend-Susan went off to their caroling.

When they came to the village they meant to sing outside Mr Blunt's corn-shop, and Miss Muggins's draper's shop; but all the little shop-windows were so brightly lit up it made them feel shy.

People were going in and out of Mr Smale the Grocer's shop, and Mrs Hubble the Baker's shop, and sometimes they stopped to look in Miss Muggins's window (which was showing a lot of gay little penny toys and strings of tinsel balls, as well as gloves and handkerchiefs).

Milly-Molly-Mandy said, "Let's wait!" and Billy Blunt said, "Come on!" So they turned into the dark lane by the forge.

They heard the *cling-clang* of a hammer banging on the anvil. And Milly-Molly-Mandy said, "Let's sing to Mr Rudge!" So they went up to the half-open door of the forge.

Billy Blunt blew a little note on the mouth-organ, and they started on their carol.

By the end of the first verse the Blacksmith was bringing his hammer down in time to the music, and it sounded just like a big bell chiming; and then he began joining in, in a big humming sort of voice. And when they finished he shouted out, "Come on in and give us some more!"

So Milly-Molly-Mandy and Billy Blunt and little-friend-Susan came in out of the dark.

It was lovely in the forge, so warm and full of strange shadows and burnt-leathery sort of smells. They had a warm-up by the fire, and then began another song. And the Blacksmith sang and hammered all to time; and it sounded – as Mr Jakes the Postman popped his head in to say – "real nice and Christmassy!"

"Go on, give us some more,'" said the Blacksmith, burying his horseshoe in the fire again to make it hot so that he could punch nail-holes in it.

"We can't do many more," said Milly-Molly-Mandy, "because the mouth-organ isn't quite big enough."

"Oh, never mind that," said the

They started on their carol

Blacksmith. "Go on, William, give us *Hark the Herald Angels Sing*!"

So Billy Blunt grinned and struck up, and everybody joined in so lustily that nobody noticed the missing top notes. While they were in the middle of it the door creaked open a little wider, and Miss Muggins's Jilly slipped in to join the fun; and later on Mr and Mrs Blunt strolled over (when they had shut up shop); and then Mr Critch the Thatcher. And soon it seemed as if half the village were in and round the old forge, singing away, song after song, while the Blacksmith hammered like big bells on his anvil, and got all his horseshoes finished in good time before the holidays.

Presently who should come in but Father! He had been standing outside for quite a time, listening with Mother and Uncle and Aunty and Mr Moggs (they had all strolled down to see what their children were up to, and stopped to join the singing).

But soon Mother beckoned to Milly-Molly-Mandy from behind Father's shoulder, and Miss Muggins peeped round the door and beckoned to Billy Blunt, and Mr Moggs to little-friend-Susan. They knew that meant bed, but for once they didn't much mind, because it would make Christmas come all the sooner!

So the carols came to an end, and the Blacksmith called out, "What about passing the hat for the carollers!"

But Billy Blunt said with a grin, "You sang, too – louder than we did!"

And little-friend-Susan said, "Every-body sang!"

And Milly-Molly-Mandy said, "We did it for love – all of us!"

And everybody said, "So we did,

now!" and wished everybody else "Happy Christmas!"

And then Milly-Molly-Mandy said, "Good night, see you tomorrow!" to Billy Blunt, and went skipping off home to bed, holding on to Father's hand through the dark.

" PEACE ON EARTH · GOODWILL TO MEN "

Milly-Molly-Mandy
Keeps House

Once upon a time Milly-Molly-Mandy was left one evening in the nice white cottage with the thatched roof to keep house.

There was something called a political meeting being held in the next village (Milly-Molly-Mandy didn't know quite what that meant, but it was something to do with voting, which was something you had to do when you grew up), and Father and Mother and Grandpa and Grandma and Uncle and Aunty all thought they ought to go to it.

Milly-Molly-Mandy said she would not

mind one bit being left, especially if she could have little-friend-Susan in to keep her company.

So Mother said, "Very well, then, Milly-Molly-Mandy, we'll have little-friend-Susan in to keep you company. And you needn't open the door if anyone knocks unless you know who it is. And I'll leave you out some supper, in case we may be a little late getting back."

Little-friend-Susan was only too pleased to come and spend the evening with Milly-Molly-Mandy. So after tea she came in; and then Father and Mother and Grandpa and Grandma and Uncle and Aunty put on their hats and coats, and said goodbye, and went off.

And Milly-Molly-Mandy and little-friend-Susan shut the door carefully after them, and there they were, all by themselves, keeping house!

"What fun!" said little-friend-Susan. "What'll we do?"

"Well," said Milly-Molly-Mandy, "if we're house-keepers I think we ought to wear aprons."

So they each tied on one of Mother's aprons.

And then little-friend-Susan said, "Now if we've got aprons on we ought to work."

So Milly-Molly-Mandy fetched a dustpan and brush and swept up some crumbs from the floor; and little-friend-Susan folded the newspaper that was lying all anyhow by Grandpa's chair and put it neatly on the shelf. And then they banged the cushions and straightened the chairs, feeling very housekeeperish indeed.

Then little-friend-Susan looked at the plates of bread-and-dripping on the table, with the jug of milk and two little mugs. And she said, "What's that for?"

And Milly-Molly-Mandy said, "That's for our supper. But it isn't time to eat it yet. Mother says we can warm the milk on the stove, if we like, in a saucepan."

"What fun!" said little-friend-Susan. "Then we'll be cooks. Couldn't we do something to the bread-and-dripping too?"

So Milly-Molly-Mandy looked at the bread-and-dripping thoughtfully, and then she said, "We could toast it – at the fire!"

"Oh, yes!" said little-friend-Susan. And then she said, "Oughtn't we to begin doing it now? It takes quite a long time to cook things."

So Milly-Molly-Mandy said, "Let's!" and fetched a saucepan, and little-friend-Susan took up the jug of milk, and then – suddenly – "Bang-bang-*bang*!" went the door knocker, ever so loudly.

"Ooh!" said little-friend-Susan, "that

did make me jump! I wonder who it is!"

"Ooh!" said Milly-Molly-Mandy. "We mustn't open the door unless we know. I wonder who it can be!"

So together they went to the door, and Milly-Molly-Mandy put her mouth to the letter-box and said politely, "Please, who are you, please?"

Nobody spoke for a moment; and then a funny sort of voice outside said very gruffly, "I'm Mr Snooks."

And directly they heard that Milly-Molly-Mandy and little-friend-Susan looked at each other and said both together – "It's Billy Blunt!" And they unlocked the door and pulled it open.

And there was Billy Blunt standing grinning on the doorstep!

Milly-Molly-Mandy held the door wide for him to come in, and she said, "Did you think we didn't know you?"

And little-friend-Susan
said, "You did give us a
jump!" And Billy Blunt
came in, grinning all
over his face.

"We're all alone,"
said Milly-Molly-
Mandy. "We're
keeping house."

"Look at our
aprons," said little-
friend-Susan.
"We're going
to cook our
suppers."

"Come on,"
said Milly-Molly-Mandy, "and we'll give
you some. May you stop?"

Billy Blunt let them pull him into the
kitchen, and then he said he'd seen Father
and Mother and Grandpa and Grandma

and Uncle and Aunty as they went past the corn-shop to the crossroads, and Mother had told him they were alone, and that he could go and have a game with them if he liked. So he thought he'd come and give them a jump.

"Take your coat off, because it's hot in here," said Milly-Molly-Mandy. "Now we must get on with the cooking. Come on, Susan!"

So they put the milk into the saucepan on the back of the stove, and then they each took a piece of bread-and-dripping on a fork, to toast it.

But it wasn't a very good "toasting fire" (or else there were too many people trying to toast at the same time). Billy Blunt began to think it was rather long to wait, and he looked at the frying-pan on the side of the stove (in which Mother always cooked the breakfast bacon), and said, "Why not put 'em in there and fry 'em up?"

Milly-Molly-Mandy and little-friend-Susan thought that was a splendid idea; so they fried all the bread-and-dripping nice and brown (and it did smell good!). When they had done it there was just a little fat left in the pan, so they looked round for something else to cook.

"I'll go and see if there're any odd bits of bread in the bread-crock," said Milly-Molly-Mandy. "We mustn't cut any, because I'm not allowed to use the bread-knife yet."

So she went into the scullery to look, and there were one or two dry pieces in the bread-crock. But she found something else, and that was – a big basket of onions! Then Milly-Molly-Mandy gave a little squeal because she had a good idea, and she took out a small onion (she knew she might, because they had lots, and Father grew them) and ran back into the kitchen with it.

And Billy Blunt, with his scout's knife, peeled it and sliced it into the pan (and the onion made him cry like anything!); and then Milly-Molly-Mandy fried it on the stove (and the onion made her cry like anything!) and then little-friend-Susan, who didn't want to be out of any fun, stirred it up, with her head well over the pan (and the onion made her cry like anything too! – at least, she managed to get one small tear out).

And the onion smelt most delicious, all over the kitchen – only it would seem to cook all black or else not at all. But you can't think how good it tasted, spread on slices of fried bread!

They all sat on the hearthrug before the fire, with plates on their laps and mugs by their sides, and divided everything as

And the onion smelt most delicious!

evenly as possible. And they only wished there was more of everything (for of course Mother hadn't thought of Billy Blunt when she cut the bread-and-dripping).

When they had just finished the last crumb the door opened and Father and Mother and Grandpa and Grandma and Uncle and Aunty came in. And they all said together, "Whatever's all this smell of fried onions?"

So Milly-Molly-Mandy explained, and when Mother had looked at the frying-pan to see that it wasn't burnt (and it wasn't) she only laughed and opened the window.

And Father said, "Well, this smell makes me feel very hungry. Can't we have some fried onions for supper too, Mother?"

Then, before Father took little-friend-Susan and Billy Blunt home, Mother gave them all a piece of currant cake with which to finish their supper; and then she started frying a panful of onions for the grown-up supper.

And Milly-Molly-Mandy (when she had said goodbye to little-friend-Susan and Billy Blunt) watched Mother very carefully, so that she should know how to fry quite properly next time she was left to keep house!

Milly-Molly-Mandy Makes a Cosy

Once upon a time Milly-Molly-Mandy went out visiting, in her best hat and new shoes and white cotton gloves. Milly-Molly-Mandy felt very proper indeed. She walked down the road, past the Moggses' cottage, past Mr Blunt's corn-shop, till she came to Miss Muggins's small shop. For Milly-Molly-Mandy was going to tea with Miss Muggins and her little niece, Jilly.

Miss Muggins's shop and the passage behind smelt so interesting – like calico and flannelette and brown paper, with faint whiffs of peppermint and raspberry-drops. (For Miss Muggins sold a few sweets too, from bottles on a shelf in her window.)

But the little sitting-room at the back of the shop smelt most of warm buttered scones and sugary cakes, for the table was all laid ready, and Miss Muggins and Jilly were waiting for her. And over the teapot in front of Miss Muggins was a most beautiful cosy, all made of odd-shaped pieces of bright-coloured silks and velvets, with loops of coloured cord on top. Milly-Molly-Mandy did like it!

After Milly-Molly-Mandy had eaten two buttered scones she couldn't help saying, "Isn't that a beautiful cosy!"

And Jilly said, "Aunty made it!"

Milly-Molly-Mandy thought how nice it would be to have such a beautiful cosy on the table at home.

When she had eaten a pink sugary cake

She couldn't help saying, "Isn't that a beautiful cosy!"

she said, "Wasn't that cosy very difficult to make?"

And Miss Muggins (who had just come back from serving a lady with a card of linen buttons and some black elastic) said, "Oh, no, it was quite easy! You ought to get your aunty to teach you feather-stitching, Milly-Molly-Mandy, so that you could make one!"

Milly-Molly-Mandy thought how nice it would be to make Mother such a beautiful cosy, but she didn't know how she could get the stuffs.

After the meal she played with Jilly and her doll's house, and when it was time to go Miss Muggins came out of the shop with a small piece of bright red satin, to start Milly-Molly-Mandy making a cosy. Milly-Molly-Mandy was pleased!

Then she thanked Miss Muggins very much for having her, and ran home to the nice white cottage with the thatched roof.

She hid the red satin in her doll's cradle, and wondered a great deal how she could get enough pieces of stuff to make a cosy.

And then, once morning, Mother turned out of her piece-bag some scraps of green ribbon, and said Milly-Molly-Mandy might have them. Milly-Molly-Mandy *was* pleased!

But as she didn't like the thought of Mother giving anything for her own secret present she looked round for something she could do in exchange for it. And she saw, behind the kitchen door, a muddy pair of Mother's shoes waiting to be cleaned. So Milly-Molly-Mandy quietly got out the boot-box and cleaned them.

So now Milly-Molly-Mandy had some red pieces and some green pieces.

And then, one afternoon, Father gave her a penny to buy some sweets. And

Milly-Molly-Mandy said, "Would you mind, Farver, if I bought something else instead, for a great secret!"

And Father didn't mind, so Milly-Molly-Mandy went to Miss Muggins's shop and bought a skein of black silk to do the feather-stitching with.

So now Milly-Molly-Mandy had some red pieces and some green pieces and a skein of black silk.

And then, one day, Grandma altered her best dress, which was of velvet, and the part she cut off she gave to Milly-Molly-Mandy to play with.

So now Milly-Molly-Mandy had some red pieces and some green pieces and a skein of black silk and some black pieces.

And then, one morning, Grandpa let her come down with him in the pony-trap to the town. And while they were there he looked at the shop windows and asked

Milly-Molly-Mandy what she would like for a little present. And Milly-Molly-Mandy said, "Oh, Grandpa, could I have some coloured cord for a great secret?" So Grandpa bought her some coloured cord without asking any questions.

So now Milly-Molly-Mandy had some red pieces and some green pieces and a skein of black silk and some black pieces and some coloured cord.

And then, one afternoon, Aunty was retrimming a hat and when she took off the old lavender ribbon it had on it she said Milly-Molly-Mandy could have it. And Milly-Molly-Mandy found some parts of it were quite good.

So now Milly-Molly-Mandy had some red pieces and some green pieces and a skein of black silk and some black pieces and some coloured cord and some lavender pieces.

And then, one day, Uncle was turning over the neckties in his drawer, and there was one blue one with yellow spots which Uncle didn't like, and he threw it to Milly-Molly-Mandy, saying, "Here, Milly-Molly-Mandy, this'll do for a doll's sash, or something."

So now Milly-Molly-Mandy had some red pieces and some green pieces and a skein of black silk and some black pieces and some coloured cord and some lavender pieces and some blue pieces with yellow spots.

And Milly-Molly-Mandy thought she really had enough now to begin the cosy!

She went to Aunty and asked if she would kindly teach her to do feather-stitching for a great secret. So Aunty showed her how to cut up the pieces and feather-stitch them together.

And then, for weeks, Milly-Molly-Mandy spent nearly all her spare time in the attic or in the barn, sewing and sewing, and never showed anyone but Aunty what she was doing.

One evening Father said, "Whatever is Milly-Molly-Mandy up to these days?"

And Mother said, "I can't think."

And Grandpa said, "I haven't seen her properly for days."

And Grandma said, "I think she's got some kind of a secret on."

And Uncle said, "I shouldn't be surprised."

But Aunty said nothing at all, and only put the tablecloth straight.

And then, just when Mother had finished laying the supper, Milly-Molly-Mandy came in with a very pink face and her hands behind her back.

Mother went to the oven to bring out a plate of hot potato-cakes. And when she turned round again, there, at her end of the table, was the most beautiful patchwork cosy keeping the cocoa-jug hot!

"Milly-Molly-Mandy!" said Mother.
She hurried to her place, while Milly-

Molly-Mandy jumped up and down, and Father and Grandpa and Grandma and Uncle and Aunty all looked on admiringly.

"Oh, Milly-Molly-Mandy!" said Mother, "what – a – *beautiful* – cosy!"

And Mother was so pleased, and Milly-Molly-Mandy was so glad she was pleased, that they just had to hug and kiss each other very hard indeed.

And the potato-cakes got almost cold, but the cocoa was just as hot as hot!

Milly-Molly-Mandy Keeps Shop

Once upon a time Milly-Molly-Mandy was walking home from school with some little friends – Billy Blunt, Miss Muggins's niece Jilly, and, of course, little-friend-Susan. And they were all talking about what they would like to do when they were big.

Billy Blunt said he would have a motor-bus and drive people to the station and pull their boxes about. Miss Muggins's Jilly said she would curl her hair and be a lady who acts for the pictures. Little-friend-Susan wanted to be a nurse with long white streamers, and push a pram with two babies in it.

Milly-Molly-Mandy wanted a shop like Miss Muggins's, where she could sell sweets, and cut pretty coloured stuff for people's dresses with a big pair of scissors. And, "Oh, dear!" said Milly-Molly-Mandy, "I wish we didn't have to wait till we had growed up!"

Then they came to Miss Muggins's shop, and Jilly said "Good-bye," and went in.

And then they came to Mr Blunt's corn-shop which was only a few steps farther on, and Billy Blunt said "Good-bye," and went in.

And then Milly-Molly-Mandy and little-friend-Susan, with their arms round each other, walked up the white road with the fields each side till they came to the Moggses' cottage, and little-friend-Susan said, "Good-bye" and went in.

And Milly-Molly-Mandy went hoppity-skipping on alone till she came to the nice white cottage with the thatched roof, where Mother was at the gate to meet her.

Next day was Saturday, and Milly-Molly-Mandy went down to the village on an errand for Mother. And when she had done it she saw Miss Muggins standing at her shop door, looking rather worried.

And when Miss Muggins saw Milly-Molly-Mandy she said, "Oh, Milly-

Molly-Mandy, would you mind running to ask Mrs Jakes if she could come and mind my shop for an hour? Tell her I've got to go to see someone on very important business, and I don't know what to do, and Jilly's gone picnicking."

So Milly-Molly-Mandy ran to ask Mrs Jakes. But Mrs Jakes said, "Tell Miss Muggins I'm very sorry, but I've just got the cakes in the oven, and I can't leave them."

So Milly-Molly-Mandy ran back and told Miss Muggins, and Miss Muggins said, "I wonder if Mrs Blunt would come."

So Milly-Molly-Mandy ran to ask Mrs Blunt. But Mrs Blunt said, "I'm sorry, but I'm simply up to my eyes in house-cleaning, and I can't leave just now."

So Milly-Molly-Mandy ran back and told Miss Muggins, and Miss Muggins said she didn't know of anyone else she could ask.

Then Milly-Molly-Mandy said, "Oh, Miss Muggins, couldn't I look after the shop for you? I'll tell people you'll be back in an hour, and if they only want a sugar-stick or something I could give it them – I know how much it is!"

Miss Muggins looked at Milly-Molly-Mandy, and then she said: "Well, you aren't very big, but I know you're careful, Milly-Molly-Mandy."

So she gave her lots of instructions about asking people if they would come back in an hour, and not selling things unless she was quite sure of the price, and so on. And then Miss Muggins put on her hat and feather boa and hurried off.

And Milly-Molly-Mandy was left alone in charge of the shop!

Milly-Molly-Mandy felt very solemn

and careful indeed. She dusted the counter with a duster which she saw hanging on a nail; and then she peeped into the window at all the handkerchiefs and socks and bottles of sweets – and she could see Mrs Hubble arranging the loaves and cakes in her shop window opposite, and Mr Smale (who had the grocer's shop with a little counter at the back where you posted parcels and bought stamps and letter-paper) standing at his door enjoying the sunshine. And Milly-Molly-Mandy felt so pleased that she had a shop as well as they.

And then, suddenly, the door-handle rattled, and the little bell over the door jangle-jangled up and down, and who should come in but little-friend-Susan! And how little-friend-Susan did stare when she saw Milly-Molly-Mandy behind the counter!

"Miss Muggins has gone out on 'portant

business, but she'll be back in an hour. What do you want?" said Milly-Molly-Mandy.

"A packet of safety-pins for Mother. What are you doing here?" said little-friend-Susan.

"I'm looking after the shop," said Milly-Molly-Mandy. "And I know where the safety-pins are, because I had to buy some yesterday."

So Milly-Molly-Mandy wrapped up the safety-pins in a piece of thin brown paper, and twisted the end just as Miss Muggins did. And she handed the packet to little-friend-Susan, and little-friend-Susan handed her a penny.

And then little-friend-Susan wanted to stay and play "shops" with Milly-Molly-Mandy.

But Milly-Molly-Mandy shook her head solemnly and said, "No, this isn't play: it's business. I've got to be very, very careful. You'd better go, Susan."

And just then the bell jangled again, and a lady came in, so little-friend-Susan went out. (She peered through the window for a time to see how Milly-Molly-Mandy got on, but Milly-Molly-Mandy wouldn't look at her.)

The lady was Miss Bloss, who lived opposite, over the baker's shop, with Mrs Bloss. She wanted a quarter of a yard of pink flannelette, because she was making a wrapper for her mother, and she hadn't bought quite enough for the collar. She said she didn't like to waste a whole hour till Miss Muggins returned.

Milly-Molly-Mandy stood on one leg and wondered what to do, and Miss Bloss tapped with one finger and wondered what to do.

And then Miss Bloss said, "That's the

roll my flannelette came off. I'm quite sure Miss Muggins wouldn't mind my taking some."

So between them they measured off the pink flannelette, and Milly-Molly-Mandy fetched Miss Muggins's big scissors, and Miss Bloss made a crease exactly where the quarter-yard came; and Milly-Molly-Mandy breathed very hard and cut slowly and carefully right along the crease to the end.

And then she wrapped the piece up and gave it to Miss Bloss, and Miss Bloss handed her half a crown, saying, "Ask Miss Muggins to send me the change when she gets back."

And then Miss Bloss went out.

And then for a time nobody came in, and Milly-Molly-Mandy amused herself by trying to find the rolls of stuff that different people's dresses had come off. There was her own pink-and-white-striped cotton (looking so lovely and new) and Mother's blue checked apron stuff and Mrs Jakes's Sunday gown . . .

Then rattle went the handle and jangle went the bell, and who should come in but Billy Blunt!

"I'm Miss Muggins," said Milly-Molly-Mandy. "What do you want to buy?"

"Where's Miss Muggins?" said Billy Blunt.

So Milly-Molly-Mandy had to explain again. And then Billy Blunt said he had wanted a penny-worth of aniseed balls. So Milly-Molly-Mandy stood on a box and reached down the glass jar from the shelf.

They were twelve a penny,

"I'm Miss Muggins. What do you want to buy?"

she knew, for she had often bought them. So she counted them out, and then Billy Blunt counted them.

And Billy Blunt said, "You've got one too many here."

So Milly-Molly-Mandy counted again, and she found one too many too. So they dropped one back in the jar, and Milly-Molly-Mandy put the others into a little bag and swung it over by the corners, just as Miss Muggins did, and gave it to Billy Blunt. And Billy Blunt gave her his penny.

And then Billy Blunt grinned, and said, "Good morning, ma'am."

And Milly-Molly-Mandy said, "Good morning, sir," and Billy Blunt went out.

After that an hour began to seem rather a long time, with the sun shining so outside. But at last the little bell gave a lively jangle again, and Miss Muggins had returned!

And though Milly-Molly-Mandy had

enjoyed herself very much, she thought perhaps, after all, she would rather wait until she was grown up before she kept a shop for herself.

Joyce Lankester Brisley

MILLY-MOLLY-MANDY'S Family

*Once upon a time there was a little
girl. She had a Father, and a Mother,
and a Grandpa, and a Grandma,
and an Uncle, and an Aunty;
and they all lived together in a nice
white cottage with a thatched roof.*

Milly-Molly-Mandy has a very big family and she
loves them all very much. Join her as she organizes a
party for her grandparents and a surprise for her
mother, runs errands for the whole family and
steals the show at the village concert!

Joyce Lankester Brisley

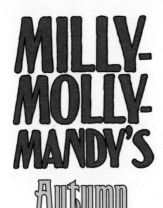

MILLY-MOLLY-MANDY'S Autumn

*Autumn is a very
busy time for
Milly-Molly-Mandy*

It's a blustery autumn and Milly-Molly-Mandy
has lots to do! Join her on Guy Fawkes Night,
discover the secret plant that is growing in
her garden and attend a wedding that
ends with a bang!

MILLY-MOLLY-MANDY'S

Things to Make and Do

Based on the stories by

JOYCE LANKESTER BRISLEY

Whether she's baking a cake, planting a
miniature garden or having a dolls' tea-party,
Milly-Molly-Mandy is always having fun.
Packed with teatime treats, crafty fun and big ideas
to brighten up a gloomy day, this is the perfect
book for long holidays, rainy days and
adventures in your own back garden!

With easy-to-follow instructions for lots of
wonderful activities, including:

❖ Baking blackberry
   crumble
❖ Sewing patchwork
❖ Knitting a scarf

❖ Planting sunflowers
❖ Identifying leaves
❖ Building a fort
❖ Making a bird feeder

And much, much more!

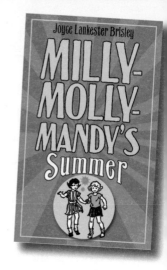

Collect them all!

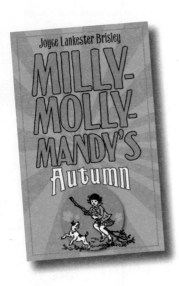

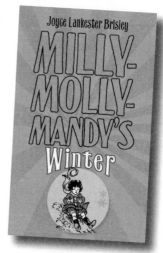

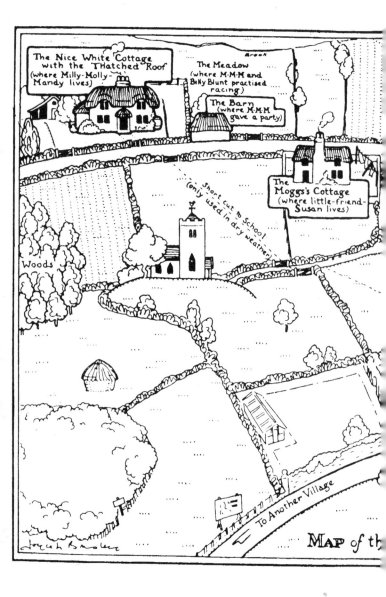